SHUTDOWN

IS THE FRUIT OF THE SPIRITUAL BREAKDOWN!

SHUTDOWN

IS THE FRUIT OF THE SPIRITUAL BREAKDOWN!

The Corona Virus is Not Just a Pandemic
but a Divine Judgment that is Apocalyptic

RULER ROBERTS JR.

ReadersMagnet, LLC

Shutdown: Is the Fruit of the Spiritual Breakdown!
Copyright © 2021 by Ruler Roberts Jr.

Published in the United States of America
ISBN Paperback: 978-1-953616-82-1
ISBN eBook: 978-1-953616-83-8

This book is written to provide information and motivation to readers. Its purpose is not to render any type of psychological, legal, or professional advice of any kind. The content is the sole opinion and expression of the author, and not necessarily that of the publisher.

All rights reserved. No part of this publication may be reproduced, stored in a retrieval system or transmitted in any way by any means, electronic, mechanical, photocopy, recording or otherwise without the prior permission of the author except as provided by USA copyright law.

ReadersMagnet, LLC
10620 Treena Street, Suite 230 | San Diego, California, 92131 USA
1.619.354.2643 | www.readersmagnet.com

Book design copyright © 2021 by ReadersMagnet, LLC. All rights reserved.
Cover design by Ericka Obando
Interior design by Renalie Malinao

CONTENTS

Chapter 1 A Shutdown is the Fruit of a Spiritual Breakdown 1
Chapter 2 The New System 7
Chapter 3 Picture of the Old and New System 10
Chapter 4 The Elect 14
Chapter 5 Babylonian Times..................... 17
Chapter 6 America – Elected to Be Perfected 21
Chapter 7 Hurricane Donald – A Sign of the Times..... 24
Chapter 8 Manifestation of the Administration (The New System) 30

About the Author 33

God first revealed the law of sowing and reaping when He created the natural world and every living thing to reproduce after its own kind. When he formed Adam, he breathed life into Adam from His own substance and nature. His design was perfect, and His pleasure in mankind was complete.

However, before the first natural conception let me say it this way for you millennials before Eve became Adam's baby mama. Their act of disobedience sowed the spiritual seed of sin and death into their lives and bodies. That seed produced the deadly harvest of which you and I are a part. Their offspring have been born after their own kind with the terminal disease of sin and death.

In other words, Adam and Eve had a breakdown or disconnect in their relationship with God that produced a shutdown or a defect in their stewardship in the Garden of Eden.

CHAPTER ONE

A SHUTDOWN IS THE FRUIT OF A SPIRITUAL BREAKDOWN

These two words, shutdown and breakdown, are similar but they are applied differently. Shutdown means to cause something as in a person, place or thing to cease, to close down, to collapse, to fail. Some examples are a president, a teacher, a doctor, or a lawyer. Place examples are a nation, a city, a kingdom, a mall, a park, a school, a car, a plane, or a train. Breakdown means a failure of a relationship or system of that person, place or thing; to depart from the principles, laws, methods of that person, place or thing; a loss of the ability to function effectively for what it was created for; a financial system, a religious system, a mechanical system, a technical system a biological system. When a car or vehicle engine breaks down, that causes the car to, guess what, shut down.

Another example is if a human body has a defect or breakdown in their physical body or biological system that causes the person's body to shut down. A shutdown is the fruit of a spiritual breakdown.

In Genesis chapter 2, verse 9, "and out of the ground the Lord God made every tree that is pleasant to the sight and good for food." "The Tree of Life was also in the midst of the garden, and the Tree of the Knowledge of Good and Evil." But of the Tree of Knowledge of Good and Evil you shall not eat, for in the day that you eat it you shall surely die" (verse 17). Shutdown! Their choice to eat of the Tree of the Knowledge of Good and Evil produced another seed/system or the system of sin and death. They became sin stain on the brain!

Deuteronomy chapter 30 verse 19 says, "I called Heaven and Earth as a witness today against you, that I have set before you life and death, blessing and cursing. Therefore, choose life, that both you and your descendants may live." Galatians chapter 6 verses 7-8: "Do not be deceived. God is not mocked, for whatsoever a man sows, that he will also reap." Verse 8: "He that sows to the flesh will of the flesh reap corruption, but he who sows to the spirit will of the spirit reap everlasting life."

Romans chapter 7 verse 5, "For when we were in the flesh, the motion of sin, which was by law, did bring forth fruit unto death." Shutdown. That defect made us subject to the law of sin and death. Remember old Lucifer – he got shut down because he had a breakdown. During the days of Noah the whole world shut down. Sodom and Gomorrah got shut down. Even Nimrod who tried to build a tower up to heaven got shut down. And on December 21, 2018, the United States of American got shut down! (See Exhibits A and B)

EXHIBIT A
Apocalyptic Prophecy on November 28, 2018

This letter is to inform you of the apocalyptic prophecies of the "Seven Day Week" in the end times that has been unsealed in the Book of Daniel. Daniel chapter 12 verse 4: "Thou oh Daniel shut up the words and seal the book even to the time of the end, many shall run to and fro and knowledge shall be increased.

As Paul said in Galatians chapter 1 verse 12, "For I neither received it from man, nor was I taught it, but it came through the revelations of Jesus Christ, which I have been gifted with the word of knowledge and the spirit of revelation. Here is the revelation.

"The Seven Day Week is determined to" make an end to sin. The definition of determined: cause something to occur in a particular way, be decisive, factor in.

Daniel chapter 9 verse 24: "70 weeks are determined upon the holy city, to finish the transgressions, and to make an end of sins, and to make reconciliations for iniquity, and to bring in everlasting righteousness, and to seal up the vision and prophecy, and to anoint the most holy." The 70 weeks = 7 days x 10.

In Genesis chapter 2 verse 3, God blessed the seventh day and sanctified it. God ordained a Sabbath day to determine the end of sin and to bring in everlasting righteousness. From Genesis two revelations, the 7-day weeks are used in the perpetual judgment in the times of man. In the Old Testament, you have atonement or condemnation. In the New Testament you have sanctification or condemnation.

Exodus chapter 12 verse 17, the seven-day Feast of unleavened bread.

Exodus 20 verse 8, remember the Sabbath day to keep it holy.

Leviticus chapter 25 verse 2, the land shall keep the Sabbath.

Leviticus chapter 25 verse 8, seven years of sevens, the Jubilee year 7 x 7.

Joshua chapter 6 verse 4, seven times around the walls of Jericho and it fell.

Judges chapter 16 verse 19, Samson's seven locks were cut and he lost his strength.

First Kings chapter 18 verse 43, Elijah in the famine sent his servants to the sea seven times looking.

Second Kings chapter 5 verse 10, Naaman dipped in the Jordan River seven times.

Jeremiah chapter 25 verse 11, 70 years in Babylonian captivity.

Nehemiah chapter 6 verse 15, rebuilt the walls in seven weeks.

Luke chapter 3 verse 23, Jesus' anointing in the Jordan River to the crucifixion 70 weeks.

Matthew 24 verse 2, Jesus teaches on the destruction of the Temple in 70 AD.

Matthew 24 verse 32 through 35: "Now learn the parable of the fig tree, when his branch is yet tender and put it for leaves, ye know that summer is nigh. So likewise ye, when you shall see all these things know that it is near even at the door." The fig tree [Israel] put forth leaves when it was reinstated as a nation in 1948 and the capital in Jerusalem 2018. We are now in the 70th year of Israel's rebirth.

The attack at the Jewish synagogue in Pittsburgh, PA, happened on the seventh day of the week, the 27th date of the month in the 70th year.

"And they were written for our admonition upon whom the end of the age has come" (distinct period).

The Seven-Day week has determined the end of sin and to bring in everlasting righteousness. Jesus Christ says He is the Alpha and the Omega – the beginning and the end. It has already been determined that a divine judgment is near, even at the door.

The Shutdown is a Divine judgment. The shutdown was a divine event which occurred in America. On Wednesday, November 28, 2018, I released a message. Its title: "The 7-day week have determined."

On 12/21/2018 American was shut down!

**Grace Ministry
Gifted Resources at Christian Excellence
Presents
An Apocalyptic Prophecy
"A Shutdown Is The Fruit"
of
A Spiritual Breakdown**

May 31, 2019 – 7:00 PM
Grace Ministry
77 NW 7th ST. Gainesville, Florida
Hosted by: Grace Ministry
Founder/Evangelist Ruler Roberts Jr.
Genesis 2:17

CHAPTER TWO

THE NEW SYSTEM

In Jeremiah chapter 7 God calls Jeremiah to warn Israel of the coming shutdown. After Israel's continued disobedience and idolatry which is a breakdown, guess what – Israel got shut down. God used wicked King Nebuchadnezzar to take Israel into captivity for 70 years.

In Jeremiah chapter 31, verses 31-33: "Behold the days are coming, says the Lord, when I will make a New Covenant with the house of Israel and with the house of Judea. Not according to the covenant that I made with their fathers in that day that I took them by the hand to bring them out of the land of Egypt, my covenant which they broke, though I was a husband to them, says the Lord. But this is the Covenant that I will make with the house of Israel after those days, says the Lord. I will put my law in their minds and write it on their hearts and I will be their God and they shall be my people. A new covenant, a new relationship. No longer do they have to do things with the blood of goats and calves, not with natural things." Now when you accept Jesus Christ as your Lord and Savior you are born of this new relationship, new system. In Romans 10 and 10, it says "for with the heart man believeth unto righteousness and with the mouth confession is made unto salvation." Now you are born again of this new system. See, being righteous does not just mean religion, but not being subject to the wrong in the world, the law of sin and death that's in the world.

Romans 4 and 8 says, "Blessed is the man that the Lord does not impute sin." Romans 6:22, "being made free from sin you become a servant of God, having your fruits on the Holiness and the end everlasting life." Romans 8 verse 2, "For the law of the spirit of life has made me free from the law of sin and death." No sin, no breakdown, no breakdown, no shutdown!

Satan wants to break down your relationship with your source to shut down your Force. Satan can't stop you. You have a new system of life in Jesus Christ. If any man be in Christ, he is a new creature – in other words, he has a new system; old things have passed away. All things have become new in the new system in Jesus Christ. Be not conformed to this world, the old system, but be ye transformed by the renewing of your mind in the new system. Greater is He, the new system that's in you, than he that's in the world, the old system. He has called you out of darkness, the old system, and into His marvelous light, the new system. We are in the world, the old system, but not of the world. We've got a new system of life in Jesus Christ.

Romans chapter 6 verse 5 says, "Just as Christ was raised from the dead, we also should walk in the newness of life" in the new system. The thing about a lot of religious folk, they think being a Christian is religion, going to the church house, singing in the choir, being on the usher board. All those things are just part of it, but Christianity means being Christlike. Taking on the qualities and character and authority in this world and having the power to not be subject to the law of the old system, sin and death. No sin, no breakdown, no breakdown, no shutdown. No sin, no disconnect, no disconnect, no defect in God's elect.

Elected to carry out the will of God in the world system which is natural and temporary. God is a spirit and eternal, so God the Father sent His Son to reproduce sons of God, the Elect. They are not subject to the world (law of sin) but subjected to the laws of God, of the spirit of life, the Spirit of God, the new system.

CHAPTER THREE

PICTURE OF THE OLD AND NEW SYSTEM

God revealed this newness of life or new system in His elect during the ancient times of Israel under King Ahab. Both the old and the new system were revealed in First Kings chapter 16 verse 33 through chapter 17 verse 21 and in the Book of Daniel he revealed the new system in the last days with his elect in the ancient times of the Babylonian captivity. Remember, He declared the end in the beginning and from the ancient times.

First Kings chapter 16 verse 33: "And Ahab made a grove and did more to provoke the Lord God of Israel to anger than all the kings of Israel that were before him.

Chapter 17 verses 1 to 6: "And Elijah the Tishbite, of the inhabitants of Gilead, said unto Ahab, as the Lord God of Israel living, before whom I stand, there shall not be dew nor rain these years, but according to my word. And the word of the Lord came unto him, saying, get thee hence, and turn the Eastward and hide thyself by the brook Cherith that is before Jordan. And it shall be that thou shall drink of the brook and I have commanded the ravens to feed thee there. So he went and did according unto the word of the Lord for he went and dwelt by the brook. And the raven brought him bread and flesh in the morning and bread and flesh in the evening and he drank of the brook.

Here in verses 4 through 6 you have a type of Old Covenant relationship or system. God always dealt with Israel on a natural level in the Old Covenant. He would deal with them on a natural level or he would use natural things to accomplish His will. For example, He used the Red Sea to destroy Pharaoh and his army. In the wilderness He used a tree that was cast into the middle of the bitter water and made it sweet. You have to ask yourself, why does God use a raven and the brook when he could have done it supernaturally like have water come from a rock.

Verse 7: "And it came to pass after a while that the brook dried up because there had been no rain in the land." This is a famine – a type of shutdown, to be without, to lack the necessities for life.

Verses 8 and 9: "And the Word of the Lord came to him saying, arise, go to Zarephath. And when he came to the gate of the city, the widow woman was there gathering sticks. And he called to her and said, fetch me I pray a little water in a vessel that I may drink." Zarephath is in Samaria. Can you think of someone else who met a widow from Samaria and asked for a drink? Yes, our Lord and Savior Jesus Christ at the well (John 19:28).

Verse 11: "And as she was going to fetch it he called to her and said, bring me I pray thee a morsel of bread in the hand."

Verse 12: "And she said, as the Lord God liveth, I have not any cake but a handful of meal in a barrel and a little oil in a cruse. And behold, I am gathering two sticks that I may go in and dress it for me and my son that we may eat it and die."

Verse 13: "And Elijah said unto her, fear not. Go and do as thou hast said but make me therefore a little cake first and bring it unto me and after that for you and the son."

Verse 14: "Father says the Lord God of Israel, the barrel of meal shall not waste, neither shall the cruse of oil, it will not fail until the day that the Lord sends rain upon the earth."

Verse 15: "And she went and did according to Elijah and she and he and her house did eat many days."

Verse 16: "And the barrel of meal wasted not neither did the cruse of oil fail according to the word of the Lord which He spoke. By Elijah."

Verse 17: "And it came to pass after these things that the son of the woman, the mistress of the house, fell sick and his sickness was so sore that there was no breath left in him."

Verse 21: "And he stretched himself upon the child three times and cried unto the Lord and said, Oh Lord, my God, I pray thee let this child's soul come into him again." The three times refers to Matthew chapter 12 verse 38, that says, "As Jonah was in the whale three days and three nights so shall the Son of Man be three days and three nights in the heart of the Earth.

Romans 8 and 11, "But if the spirit of Him who raised Jesus from the dead dwells in you, He who raised Christ from the dead will also give life to your mortal body through His Spirit who dwells in you." Hallelujah! Praise the Lord. This is the newness of Life – a new system of life.

In verses 1 through 4 you have a picture of the old system. God used natural things. In verses 5 through 21, the new system, by faith system.

CHAPTER FOUR

THE ELECT

Daniel chapter 1 verse 1: "In the third year of the reign of Jehoiakim King of Judah, came Nebuchadnezzar, king of Babylon, to Jerusalem and besieged it."

Verse 2: "And the Lord gave Jehoiakim, king of Judea, into his hand with part of the vessels of the house of God which he carried into the land of Shinar to the house of God. And he brought the vessels into the treasure house of his god.

Verse 3: "And the king spoke unto Ashpenaz the master of his eunuchs that he should bring certain of the children of Israel and of the king's seed and of the princes." In this verse you have the king's seed, the elect of God "elected to be perfection."

Verse 11: "And whosoever falls not down and worships that he should be cast into the midst of the burning fiery furnace."

Verse 16: "Shadrach, Meshach and Abednego answered and said, See if we are not careful to answer thee in this matter."

Verse 17: "If it be so our God whom we serve is able to delivery us from the burning fiery furnace and He will deliver us out of thy hand, o king."

Verse 22: "Therefore because the king's command was urgent and the furnace exceeding hot the flames of the fire slew those men that took up the three Hebrew boys."

Verse 23: "And these three men fell down bound into the midst of the burning fiery furnace."

Verse 24: "Then the king was astonished and rose up in haste and spake and said unto his counselors, did not we cast three men down into the midst of the fire? They answered and said unto the king, true, O king."

Verse 25: "He answered and said, lo, I see four men loose walking in the midst of the fire and they have no hurt and the form of the fourth is like the Son of God."

In verse 25 it doesn't say that the fourth one said or did anything. The fourth one was there to show the form of the Son of God and how God's elect conform to the form or image of Jesus Christ. The fire is a type of sin or corruption. This is a picture of the end time when there shall be perilous times in the last days and God's elect will be able to stand in the fire of sin and corruption.

Second Peter chapter 1 verse 4, "But which have been given to us exceedingly great and precious promises that through these you may be partakers of a divine nature having escaped the corruption that is in the world through lust. The three Hebrew boys had conformed into the image of Christ to have power and authority over the natural world or the laws of sin and death. They were not subject to the evil that he tried to destroy them with.

Romans 8:28 says, "All things work together for good to them that love the Lord, them that are called according to His purpose for whom He foreknew He also predestined to be conformed to the image of His Son that he might be the firstborn among many brethren.

Moreover, whom He predestined these He also called and those He called He also justified and those He justified He also glorified. What then shall we say to these things? If God be for us, who can be against us? He who did not spare His own Son but delivered Him up for us all, how shall He not with Him also freely give us all things? Who shall bring a charge against God's elect?" Elected to be perfected.

Verse 35: "Who shall separate us from the love of Christ? Shall tribulation or distress or persecution or famine or nakedness or peril or sword?"

Verses 37 to 39: "Yet in all these things we are more than conquerors through Him who loved us. For I am persuaded that neither death nor life nor angels nor principalities nor powers nor things present nor things to come, nor height nor depth nor any other created thing shall be able to separate us from the love of God which is in Christ Jesus our Lord." Praise the Lord!

They changed the country but that didn't change their character. They changed the food but that didn't change their faith. The changed their names but that didn't change their nature. They had become Christ-like, conformed into His image. This was the New Covenant system, the new relationship, the new way. You don't need to go to a priest and have the priest go into the temple and ask for your blessing to ask for your prayers to ask for the things that you need. You now can go boldly before the Throne of God as sons of God in His Name, the One that was in the flame with them, our Lord and Savior Jesus Christ. They were in the fire but not of the fire.

CHAPTER FIVE

BABYLONIAN TIMES

That same haughty spirit that was in ancient Babylon during the time of Israel's captivity is now in America. President Trump and King Nebuchadnezzar have the same haughty spirit. That President Trump is a picture or type of that king is now being revealed. Remember God declared the end in the beginning and from ancient times.

In Jeremiah chapter 25 verse 9, God calls the king His servant. He used him to bring Israel into captivity for 70 years. He used President Trump to reinstate the capital of Israel by moving it back to Jerusalem in the 70th year of the rebirth of Israel (1949). Proverbs chapter 21 verse 1: "The king's heart is in His hands as rivers of running water; He turns it whichever way He will." President Trump is making Babylon great in America. Here are more comparisons:

The king carried Israel into captivity. The President carried the evangelical vote.

The king was the most powerful king on earth during his time. The President sits in the most powerful seat on earth.

The king built an image of himself with gold. The President built Trump Tower and now wants to build a wall for a monument to himself.

The king made a decree that everyone must fall down and worship his image. The President made a tweet that NFL players must stand for the image of the American flag.

The king cast three Hebrew boys into the fiery furnace. The President said NFL players should be fired.

The king declared Israel's God is God. The President declared Jerusalem is the capital of Israel.

The king said, "I have built the kingdom by my power." The President said, "I alone can make America great again."

This is not a campaign between Democrats and Republicans, conservatives versus liberals, but a spiritual conflict between the spirit of truth and the spirit of error. Good vs. Evil. The law of the spirit of life versus the law of sin and death, light versus darkness. You have to discern what is happening in America spiritually but the "talking heads" see it through the world system or with their intellect. This is a spiritual warfare. Here's a description the Bible says in Second Timothy chapter 3 verse 1: "But know this, in the last days perilous times will come."

Verse 2: "For men will be lovers of themselves, lovers of money, boasters, proud, blasphemers, disobedient to parents, unthankful, unholy."

Verse 3: "unloving, unforgiving, slanderous, without self-control, brutal, despisers of good."

Verse 4: "Trailers, headstrong, hardy. Love is a pleasure rather than lovers of God."

Verse 5: "Having a form of godliness but denying its power. And from such people turn away."

In First Timothy chapter 4 verse 1, "In latter times some shall depart from the faith, giving heed to seducing spirits and doctrines of devils speaking lies in hypocrisy, having their conscience seared with a hot iron."

This is the Babylonian spirit that you are now seeing in America: Babel, which means confusion. The followers of Trump will accept anything that he says. Here's why: Thessalonians chapter 2 verse 10, "And with all unrighteousness deceptions among those who perish because they did not receive the love of the truth that they might be saved."

Verse 11: "And for this reason God will send them strong delusion, that they should believe the lie."

Verse 12: "That they all may be condemned who did not believe the truth but had pleasure in unrighteousness."

Isn't this what you're seeing today in America? The lawlessness, the people in Trump's cabinet all have become corrupt, then he cast them by the wayside or fired and abused them with his language.``

You discern a tree by the fruit it bears. You don't get sweet water from a bitter well. If the well is bitter you get bitter water. Jesus Himself prophesied in Matthew chapter 24 verse 15 about this lawless one. "Therefore when you see the abomination of desolation spoken of by Daniel the Prophet standing in the holy place." He also said there be many Antichrists that will come. Remember these two are types – a metaphor – the real Antichrist will be Satan himself manifested on earth. What this does is it lets us know that we are in the season. No man knows the day or the hour, but the season.

In Daniel chapter 4 verse 30, the king speaks, "See is not this great Babylon that I have built for the house of the kingdom by the might of my power and for the honor of my majesty?"

Verse 31: "While the word was in the king's mouth there fell a voice from heaven saying, O King Nebuchadnezzar, to thee it is spoken that the kingdom is departed from thee."

Verse 32: "And they shall drive you from men and thy dwelling shall be with the beast and they shall make you to eat grass as oxen and seven times shall pass over you until I know that the Most High rules in the kingdom of men and gave it to whomsoever He will." So shall it be with President Trump. Proverbs 29 verse 23: "A man's pride shall bring him low."

Verse 29: "Many seek the ruler's favor, but judgment comes from the Lord."

There is a penalty for corruption/sin. Sometimes in a nation you have to commit civil disobedience to a king in order to obey the King of Kings and God our Father and Savior Jesus Christ and do what is right.

Trump can't win because of sin. Racism and egotism is sin. The instinct impulse is in all of us but if it goes unharnessed it is dangerous. It causes a disconnect and brings a defect in our personality. It distorts it. Some say it is more dangerous than sex. There have been many men who had an out-of-control impulse: men like the Pharaohs of Egypt, Haman, King Herod, Adolf Hitler, Mao Zedong, Kim Jong un, Charles Manson. All these men had a similar personality disorder: they all wanted to be worshipped. Does this not sound familiar? They wanted to push others down to lift themselves up. So when you have the head of a nation, a king, a president or a dictator with these qualities, the whole nation will suffer.

America has always been a blessed nation because it was founded on the Judean Christian values and principles, but America has become broken and disconnected. The country was strong when it had a leader who morally adhered to the Word of God.

CHAPTER SIX

AMERICA – ELECTED TO BE PERFECTED

God told Israel the same thing He had done in the beginning when He created the world. Genesis chapter 2 verse 3, "And God blessed the seventh day and sanctified it because in it He had rested from all His work which God had created and made."

Leviticus 25 verse 2: "Speak unto the children of Israel and say to them, when you come into the land which I give you, then shall the land keep a Sabbath unto the Lord."

Verse 3: "Six years thou shalt sow fields and six years prune the vineyards and gather in the fruit thereof."

Verse 4: "But in the seventh year shall be a Sabbath of rest unto the Lord, a Sabbath for the Lord. Thou shall neither sow nor harvest the vineyard."

These were the divine laws of establishment on which the Constitution was written to make Israel and America a divine nation, his elect.

It was George Washington who stated, "Do not let anyone claim to be a true American if they ever attempt to remove religion from politics."

Andrew Jackson said, "The Bible is the rock on which the Republic rests."

John Adams said, "The general principles on which the fathers achieved independence were the general principles of the divine laws of establishment – Ten Commandments."

America's Supreme Court in 1892 stated our laws and our institution must necessarily be based upon the teaching of the Redeemer of mankind. Our civilization and our institution are emphatically Christian.

The national motto established by Congress in 1956 is, "In God we trust" and "God bless America." With all these fine sentiments and principles of our forefathers and founders, how can America exist today with the leadership that is now in office?

Like Israel, disobedience brought judgment from God at Shiloh by the Philistines (First Samuel chapter 4 verse 10).

And 70 years in captivity in Babylon (Daniel chapter one).

And sent fiery serpents among the people and they bit the people and much of the people of Israel died (Numbers chapter 21 verse 6).

So has judgment come to America: events like 9/11, the Murphy Building bombing, Columbine High School, Parkland High School, Sandy Hook Elementary School, Las Vegas shooting, the Orlando Pulse nightclub, El Paso Texas, Odessa Texas, fires out West, hurricanes in the East. This is not normal. There has never been a time like these times. That's why the Bible calls it perilous times.

Even now we have a spiritual hurricane known as "Donald." It is righteousness that exalts a nation, pride goeth before destruction, wealth gotten by vanity is soon diminished. It is obvious that the moral fabric of America today is where the morality of the ancient empires that ruled the world in the Dark Ages was. America has claimed that it is the world power of today. Throughout history God has always used that nation for his will.

CHAPTER SEVEN

HURRICANE DONALD – A SIGN OF THE TIMES

Matthew chapter 16, verses 1-4: "The Pharisees also with the Sadducees came, tempting Him that He would show them a sign from heaven. He answered and said unto them, when it is evening you say it will be fair weather for the sky is red. And in the morning, it will be foul weather today for the sky is red and lowering. Oh, ye hypocrites! Ye can discern the face of the sky but can you not discern the sign of the times?"

First of all, let's start with the word "sign." Sign means something that indicates a fact, conveys information, an act that is happening or even that reveals the Divine knowledge.

The Pharisees could discern the face of the sky or natural things but they could not discern the sign of the times, the spiritual things. In other words, what these acts or events mean according to the Word of God. Let's put it another way: the

Pharisees could discern the face of a storm or hurricane but they could not tell you about the face of the law of sin of "her" – Eve and Cain. I know you are asking, why do I say Eve and Cain. First Timothy chapter 2 verse 14, "And Adam was not deceived but Eve, but the woman being deceived fell into transgression."

Genesis chapter 4 verse 8, Cain slew his brother, then (verse 12), "a fugitive and vagabond you shall be on the earth." Eve committed the first sin and Cain the first homicide, so you have "her" and "Cain." And it happened to rhyme with hurricane. This was conflict. Genesis 3:15, "And I will put enmity between thee and the woman and between thy seed and her seed. It shall bruise thy head and thou shalt bruise His heel."

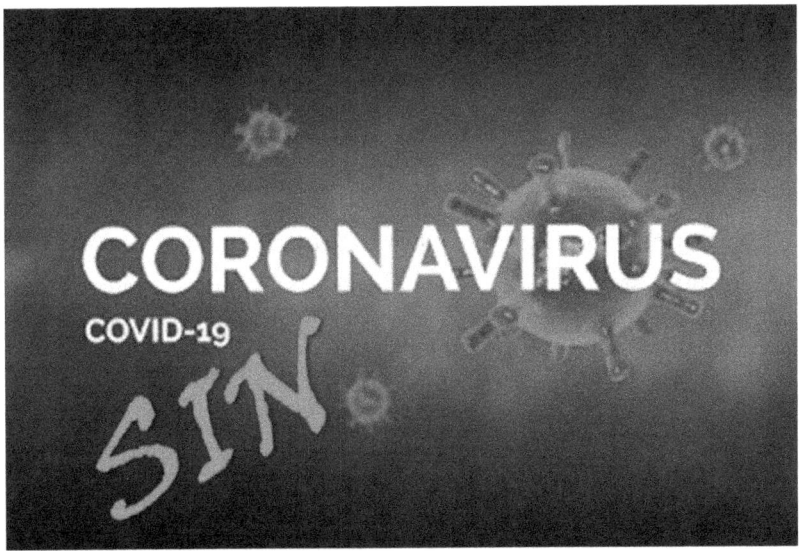

And God told Adam in Genesis 3:17-19, "Cursed is the ground. Thorns and thistles shall that bring forth. For from the dust thou are and to the dust thou shalt return." These were the consequences for the sin of her and Cain.

Foul weather in verse 3 (Matthew 16) is a type of hurricane and the description of a hurricane is a violent cyclonic storm and outbursts – a conflict between the elements of nature such as wind and rain. But there are other types of outbursts that are conflicts, such as Paul says in Romans 7 verse 19, "For the good that I would I do not, but the evil that I would not, that I do. Now if I do that I would not it is no more I that do it but sin that dwelleth in me." Donald Trump is a type of hurricane. He is in conflict with the truth. That's why you see so much corruption. You discern a tree by the fruit it bears. He is a picture of the lawless one Paul spoke about in Second Thessalonians chapter 2 verses 9-12, "The coming of the lawless one is according to the workings of Satan with all power, signs and lying wonders. And with all unrighteous deceptions among those who perished because they did not receive the love of the truth that they might be saved. And for this reason God will send them strong delusions that they should believe the lie that they all may be condemned who did not believe the truth but had pleasure in unrighteousness."

God always reveals things to his elect by giving us a type or an example of what is to come. Hurricane Donald is a revelation of the Antichrist, the lawless one, the man of sin that is to come. There have been other types of pictures of the lawless one. There was Pharaoh of Egypt who tried to kill all the first-born males in Egypt. King Nebuchadnezzar of Babylon (see chapter 5), and King Herod. They all had a conflict with Jesus.

There are other types of hurricanes/spiritual conflicts which are signs of the times:

The terrorists who flew the planes on 9/11 had a conflict with Christians and America.

Ted Bundy had a conflict with females.

John Wayne Gacy had a conflict with little boys. Dylann Roof had a conflict with black people.

The AIDS virus and cancer are in conflict with the human body.

Drug abuse is in conflict with the body and spirit. The sign is in the times.

You can recognize the face of the sky but you cannot recognize the spiritual conflict that hit Parkland High.

You can recognize the face of the Orlando Magic but cannot recognize the face of the hurricane that hit the Pulse Nightclub that was the Orlando tragic.

You can discern the face of the elementary school called Sandy Hook but cannot discern the face of the hurricane or spiritual conflict that caused 20 children to be taken.

You can discern the face of the city called Las Vegas but you cannot discern the face of the hurricane that caused the loss of 59 people in Vegas.

God said there would be no sign but the sign of Jonah. Even though Jonah was in conflict with God, God preserved him and provided a whale to swallow him up in the storm. Jonah was one of God's elect. He had been called to go to a city called Nineveh, but he was trying to go his own way. That disobedience brought the curse or a conflict, a storm or a hurricane. You notice when the hurricane came, they tried to make preparation for the wind and the rain. They were making preparation for a natural disaster rather than the Lord and Master. Don't you know God can get in any storm and get you out. He can pull the clouds back and push the sun out to a beautiful day. Jesus rebuked the hurricane when He was asleep in the belly of the boat. He said, "Peace, be still," and everything became calm.

Even though Jonah was in conflict with God by his disobedience God used that event of his three days and three nights in the belly of the whale to reveal His three days and three nights in the belly of the earth. Jonah's situation was a revelation of Jesus' resurrection. The Pharisees could not discern the sign of the times. Today the Pharisees of our time do not see the sign of the times. First Corinthians chapter 2 verses 7-10, "But we speak the wisdom of God in a mystery, the hidden wisdom which God ordained before the ages for our glory, which none of the rulers of this age knew for had they known they would not have crucified the Lord of glory. But as it is written, eyes have not seen, near ears heard nor have entered the heart of man the things which God has prepared for those who love Him. But God has revealed them to us through His Spirit."

The Spirit searches all things, yes, he deep things of God. Therefore you must be born of the Spirit of God to receive the revelations of God.

Verses 11-14: "For what man knows the things of man except the spirit of the man which is in him. Even so no one knows the things of God except the Spirit of God. But the natural man does not receive the things of the Spirit of God, for they are foolishness to him." Neither can he know them because they are spiritually discerned.

There is your answer. Here is a picture of the news headlines of today that reveals the perilous times in America. Two types of hurricanes/conflicts, they both have the same result. This is a "sign of the times."

CHAPTER EIGHT

MANIFESTATION OF THE ADMINISTRATION (THE NEW SYSTEM)

Matthew chapter 16 verse 13-15: "When Jesus came into the coast of Caesarea at Philippi, He asked his disciples saying, whom do men say that I the Son of Man am? And they said, some say that thou art John the Baptist, some others Jeremiah or one of the prophets. He said unto them, but who say ye that I am?"

They could not discern that this was the Son of God, Jesus Christ.

Verses 16-19: "And Simon Peter answered and said, Thou art the Christ, the Son of the living God. And Jesus answered and said unto him, blessed art thou, Simon bar Jonah, for flesh and blood has not revealed it unto thee but my Father which is in heaven."

This is the New Covenant, the new system that had been prophesied in Jeremiah 30 and 31: the manifestation of the administration for God's elect.

Then in verse 18, "And I say also unto thee, thou art Peter and upon this Rock I will build my church and the gates of hell shall not prevail against it."

Verse 19, "And I will give unto thee the keys of the kingdom of heaven and whatsoever thou shalt bind on earth shall be bound in heaven and whatsoever thou shalt loose on earth shall be loosed in heaven."

These scriptures here show that the Word had become flesh and dwelt among us, full of grace and truth. The Word was now standing before His disciples and Peter was being elected to be the Rock upon which Christ would build His Church and give his keys to administer His authority in the earth in the new system. The word covenant means relationship and one of the words for relationship is a system, the way you do something. Now the disciples and the sons of God His elect would be able to do the things that Christ did on earth. That's why Jesus said, "When you pray Our Father who are in heaven, Hallowed be Thy Name, Thy kingdom come in the earth," they were elected by God and perfected by the Son of God, Jesus Christ our Lord and Savior.

Acts chapter 2 verse 4, "And they were all filled with the Holy Ghost and began to speak with other tongues as the Spirit gave them utterance."

Chapter 3 verses 1-6, "Now Peter and John went up together into the Temple at the hour of prayer, being the ninth hour. And a certain man, lame from his mother's womb, was carried and lay daily at the gate of the temple which is called Beautiful, to ask alms of them that entered into the temple, who, seeking Peter and John about to go into the temple, asked for alms. And Peter, fastening his eyes upon him with John, said, look on us. And he gave heed unto them, expecting to receive something of them. Then Peter said, silver and gold have I none, but such as I have give I thee. In the Name of Jesus of Nazareth, rise up and walk."

Peter was saying natural things, the things of this world, material things I don't have, but what I do have is a new system of life. Everything that pertains to life and godliness because they were now partakers of a divine nature. It doesn't say that they had to pray or call the church members to come together to lay hands on, but he said, what I do have in the Name of Jesus of Nazareth, rise up and walk. He confessed his faith because he believed in his heart in Jesus who had given them the keys.

Verse 7: "And he took him by the right hand and lifted him up and immediately his feet and ankle bones received strength and he, leaping up, stood and walked and entered with them into the temple, walking and leaping and praising God." Hallelujah! They were elected to be perfected, to help those that had been defective (by sin and corruption).

Jesus said in Matthew 24 and 15, "When ye therefore shall see the abomination of desolation spoken of by Daniel the prophet standing in the Holy Place (whosoever readeth let him understand)." Today in the world system we now see a picture of that abomination at work in the world system. that's why God gave his elect a new system to administer His will in the last days and time.

ABOUT THE AUTHOR

Evangelist Ruler Robert, Jr., is the founder of Grace Ministry, Gifted Resources at Christian Excellence according to Ephesians 4:7. "But to each one of us grace was given according to the measure of the gift of Christ."

Ruler is gifted with the Word of Knowledge and the Spirit of Revelation, and now producing that fruit. He has been witnessing by speaking and writing to reveal the mysteries of the true knowledge of the kingdom of God.

Elected to Be Perfected Elected by God
Perfected by Jesus

Who shall bring any charge against God's elect? It is God who justifies.

Who shall separate us from the love of Christ? Shall tribulation, or distress, or persecution, or famine, or nakedness, or peril or sword?

Yet in all these things we are more than conquerors through Him who loves us.

Declaring the end from the beginning and form ancient times the things that are not yet done, my counsel shall stand, and I will do all my pleasure. (Isaiah 46:10)

Grace Ministries
Gifted Resource at Christian Excellence

www.ingramcontent.com/pod-product-compliance
Lightning Source LLC
LaVergne TN
LVHW020447080526
838202LV00055B/5372